SillyLittleStories

Stories by PJ Cowan

Illustrations by Jasen Strong

S0-APM-028

The Little Grey Rock
The Traveling Oak Leaf
The Fickle Fountain
The Reluctant Caterpillar
The Bossy Bedbug
The Scrub Jay & Spike the Cat

Edited and printed by Mira Digital Publishing.

TheLittleGreyRock

Once upon a time, there was a little grey rock. It had been sitting in a gravel path for a very long time. One day the little grey rock got tired of sitting in the path surrounded by other colorless rocks, so it jumped into the shoe of a passing child, hoping for an adventure.

The child did not like the rock in his shoe because it hurt his foot, so he took the rock and threw it into a pond. As it was sinking to the bottom of the pond, a fish saw it, decided it must be food, and swallowed the little grey rock.

Just then, an angler came by, caught the fish, and took it home to feed his family. As he was preparing the fish for cooking, the angler found the little grey rock. "Hmm," the angler said. "I wonder how that got here." He threw the rock out the window and into the garden.

The gardener found the little grey rock. "What are you doing here?" the gardener asked the rock.

"I got tired of sitting in the boring grey road," the rock replied. "Could I please stay here in the garden where everything is green?" he asked.

The Gardner took pity on the little grey rock and put it back into the garden, where it still lives, in a sea of beautiful flowers and colorful stones.

Don't be afraid to jump into a shoe that will carry you away from the boring grey road.

O nce upon a time, on the branch of a great oak tree, new little oak   leaves sprouted. As spring turned to summer and the oak leaves grew, their color turned from light green to dark green. In the fall, they turned a rich red color.

One day the strong fall wind tore all of the leaves from the trees and scattered them about the ground. One big oak leaf tumbled across the grass, across the road and down the street, finally coming to rest against a white picket fence.

As Little Johnny was walking to school, he saw the bright red oak leaf resting there by the fence. "What a beautiful leaf," Johnny thought. He leaned down, picked it up and tucked it into his storybook.

When Johnny got to school, he took the bright red oak leaf out of his book and showed it to the class. The children loved the leaf and so it passed from hand to hand, traveling all around the room for everyone to see.

Johnny shared the simple beauty of the little red leaf with his class. There is beauty all around us in flowers, a sunset or storm clouds. When you see something beautiful, share it.

TheFickleFountain

Once there was a fountain with five basins. It was tall and stately and the sparkling water made wonderful sounds as it tumbled over the edge of the high basins into the basins below.

People came from everywhere to hear the wonderful sound the fountain made. The fountain was fickle. It loved all the attention, but it didn't like folks putting their hands in its cool waters. It didn't like it when children threw coins. In short, it didn't really like people.

It did appreciate the birds that came to bathe, and the animals that came to drink its crystal clear water. One day, the fountain devised a plan. When the people came by, it splashed its waters on them, or stopped its pump so they could no longer enjoy the fountain's soothing sounds.

After a while, people grew tired of the splashing and the way the pump went on and off, so they stopped coming to see the fountain. The fountain's owner stopped cleaning it since there were no more coins to gather. The birds and animals did not come by to bathe and drink anymore, because the water was no longer clean and clear.

Now, the fickle fountain sits in the corner of the garden, sad and neglected, all because he was stubborn and would not learn to get along with people.

The Reluctant Caterpillar

Once upon a time, a small green caterpillar sat on a leaf and watched in horror as his beautiful butterfly mother was eaten by a bird. The caterpillar decided there and then that he would never become a butterfly.

He needed to figure out how to avoid the fate of his mother. He thought and thought, and finally came up with a plan. He would hide. What a great idea! he thought, giggling as he wrapped himself in a snug cocoon to hide.

The caterpillar will become a butterfly. That's who he is. We can't hide from who we really are.

The Bossy Bedbug

Once there was a bedbug, snugly settled in a mattress in the mountain cabin of Wild Willy, the trapper. Wild Willy didn't sleep in the cabin often; he much preferred sleeping outdoors under the stars. So, most of his life the bedbug had that mattress all to himself.

One chilly night in late autumn, Willy got cold so he decided to sleep indoors.
As he settled into the mattress, the bossy bedbug climbed up on Willy's hand, stood as
tall as he could and shouted in his loudest voice, "Hey, this is my mattress! You can't sleep
here!" Well, of course Willy couldn't hear the tiny creature, but he could see it, so he took
the pesky insect between his two strong trapper fingers and squished him.

Willy was lucky the bedbug was so bossy. If Willy hadn't seen him, the bedbug would have moved his wife in, raised a family there and Willy would never have been able to sleep in that bed again.

Don't buy an old used mattress unless you are willing to share it with a large family of bedbugs!

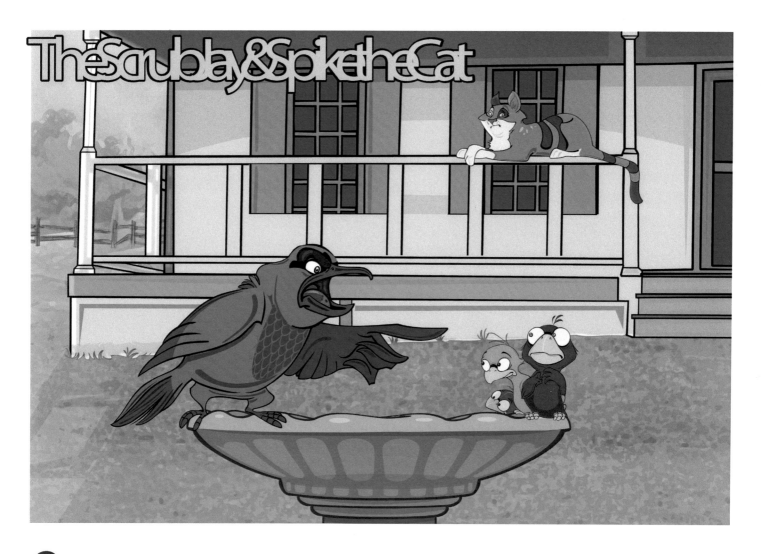

The Scrub Jay & Spike the Cat

Once upon a time, a noisy Scrub Jay lived in a tree by Grandma's house. The Jay thought he owned the whole backyard, and refused to share it with other birds or with Grandma's cat Spike.

Spike sat on the porch and watched as Jay chased the smaller birds away from the bird feeder and hogged the cool water in the birdbath. Spike was patient with the Scrub Jay because he understood that Jays are bullies. They are selfish, high-strung, and not at all easy to get along with.

One day Jay decided that the cat had to go, so he came up with a plan to get rid of the cat. Jay decided to bully the cat. He thought that if he harassed Spike long enough, Spike would get tired of it and leave the yard to him.

Every day Jay waited in the tree until Spike came into the yard, then he would dive-bomb the cat, coming as close to Spike's head as he could while screeching loudly.

The patient cat put up with this as long as he could, but one day Spike had had enough. He stood his ground, and when Jay came close to his head, Spike reached up and swatted the bird with all his might. In the end, it was Jay who moved out of the neighborhood.

Jay learned that no matter how big or how tough you are, there is always someone out there who is bigger and tougher than you are. And it is a good idea to learn to get along with your neighbor.

AbouttheIllustrator

Jasen Strong, a graphics artist and design veteran, created several children books, logos, web designs, feature films and has been a keynote speaker. He is a prominent artist in the animation & illustration industry.

http://jasenstrong.artstooge.com

About the Author

Silly Little Stories is nineteenth in a series of books written for children. These stories, wonderfully illustrated by Jasen Strong, are very short, fun and silly. Your children will love them.

See more PJ Cowan books at www.storiesbypj.com

Download to e-book on Kindle or PDF file for computer at www.e-junkie.com/pjcowan